Story by RUTH KRAUSS

The Happy Egg

Pictures by CROCKETT JOHNSON

HARPER
An Imprint of HarperCollins*Publishers*

The Happy Egg

 For information address HarperCollins Children's Books, a division of HarperCollins Publishers, 195 Broadway, New York, NY 10007.
www.harpercollinschildrens.com

Library of Congress Cataloging-in-Publication Data

Krauss, Ruth.
The happy egg. / Story by Ruth Krauss ; pictures by Crockett Johnson.
Summary: A bird hatches from its egg and learns to fly.
ISBN 978-0-06-243031-1
[1. Birds—Fiction.]
PZ10.3.K87Har5 2005 72186887
[E] CIP
AC

Typography by Neil Swaab
15 16 17 18 19 SCP 10 9 8 7 6 5 4 3 2 1
❖
Revised edition, 2016
Originally published by Scholastic Inc., in 1967.

There was a little little bird.

It was just born.
It still was an egg.

It couldn't walk.
It couldn't sing.
It couldn't fly.

It could just get sat on.

So it got sat on
and sat on

and sat on
and sat on

and sat on
and sat on
and sat on

and sat on.

And one day,

peep

POP! Out it came.

It could walk.

It could sing.

It could

fly.

It could someday sit on
other happy eggs.